CW00869180

Her Powerful Gift

By Aaliyah C

ISBN: 978-1-257-08117-2

This book is dedicated to ex-friends, and my teachers.

Introduction

Once… every 8 million years- or is it just 8 years? Let me try that again, eh-em. Once every 8 years a boy and a girl are born with a power that is incredibly powerful. Unfortunately, due to the big old boring system (yes that's actually the name of the system, B.O.B.S) the boy and girl do not know each other. If they ever meet (which is literally impossible) one of them will be able to grant their most desired wish. Although, there is a specific method that you use to grant the wish but nobody knows it. Honestly, they probably never will discover the method, it's just too complicated for any girl or boy to solve.

Table Of Contents

CHAPTER 1

~Jasmine's Backstory~

When I was born, the doctors said that there was something wrong with me, they didn't know what exactly, but they said that my pulse felt different. Till I was 5 I had to go to the doctor's office to see what was wrong with me. F.Y.I: I absolutely DESPISE going to the doctor. Literally every day the doctors would draw my blood, which hurt really bad; then took me to this dark room with a few crooked lights and asked me questions. I'd always hear my mom and the doctors talking and going down the list of things I could possibly have. Autism? No. Ticks? No. Cancer? No. Arthritis? No. Unaware of what's wrong with me? Yes.

Fast forward to when I turned 7. I loved to draw, and still do till this day. It was my birthday and I drew my mom my dream birthday cake just for fun. I colored it in, added special effects, and truly made it look amazing. Later on, when my dad came home with all of my birthday presents, a tiny man knocked on our door. He kind of looked like Bob from Bob's furniture store but in real life. My mom answered the door and he said "I heard that there is a birthday girl in this house? Well, in case that's true, I am the founder of Cakery's Bakery and I brought you a baked cake!" Within a few minutes, my mom thought about it and accepted the cake. Can you guess what happened next? It looked exactly like what I drew. It was a vanilla ice cream cake with pretty fondant flowers all around the top of the cake, and in the middle of the cake it had the number "7". Also, at the bottom of the cake there was a golden glitter drizzle, I suppose he did that to give it more bedazzle. Whatever cake you're picturing in your head is most likely what it actually was, but prettier.

When my mom placed the cake down, she stared at me, then my drawing, then the cake. Then back at the drawing and back at the cake. The back-and-forth staring went on for 10 minutes straight. Then my mom said, "Hun, d-did you know about this?" Her voice was trembling, which made me extremely scared. I shook my head no and told her I'd be right back. I raced to my room. I took a piece of paper and my favorite sharpies and drew a rainbow. I then ran back downstairs and looked outside and a rainbow appeared. The only problem was that it was snowing outside. About 10 minutes later the news weather forecast blasted loud on the TV. There was one caucasian lady with blonde hair and a tall guy with blackish hair. The meteorologists' started to talk extremely loud and said stuff like "How did this happen? Why did this happen? Who did this?" When my mom and dad heard the meteorologists' saying this, they came by the window to see for themselves and the rainbow. They were so shocked and started to catch on that something was wrong with me, but in a good way. I have…powers?

From then on, my mom took away my privileges to touch paper and writing materials and said she'll give them back when I'm older.

CHAPTER 2

Hello! My name is Jasmine but my mom and friends call me Jazzy. So basically today is going to be my first day in high school. Unfortunately for me, I missed my bus, so I've been chasing it. On the bright side, I've been chasing it for so long that I can't see my house anymore. Which means I'm getting close to school! Just a few more steps and... I can see school! While running up the stairs my best friends, Mia and Charlotte approach me, with paint canvases and paint brushes. "Hey girl!" Mia said. "Hey! How's your weekend been?" I replied. Both of the females replied with "pretty good!" "While It was the weekend Mia and I went out and got us some paint supplies! Its super aesthetic now." Charlotte smiled as her long, sunkissed-blonde hair blew in the wind. "Wow! That sounds amazing! But I don't wanna be late for class so... I'll meet you both at the back of the school during lunch and free period?" I asked. "Sounds like a plan" Mia laughed. "Alright cya then!" Charlotte waved.

As I'm walking to the first period, I get a text from my mom. I think she's mad at me because the text was in boldface letters.

CHAPTER 3

THE TEXT

I use my code, 1,12,5,24 to unlock my phone and go to messages and my mom texted me this:

Mom: "I NEED YOU TO COME HOME BEFORE LUNCH STARTS."

Me: "Okay mom."

Why does she want me to come home so early? Lunch is in like 3 hours! And I wanted to hang out with Mia and Charlotte. Ugh! Just great.

I walk into Mr. Beckette's class with my head hanging low, knowing that I'm late. "Care to explain why you're 20 minutes late for my class, Miss Jasmine Johnson?" Mr. Beckette says as he puckers his lips with his hand on his hip as if he's an old lady. I hate when he uses my last name and my first name, why do you have to let the whole world know that

I'm late? "Sorry, Mr. Beckette, I was held up." I nervously chuckle, still staring at the floor. I then take a seat at my desk, knowing that the whole class is staring at me. "Way to start the year as a freshman, Great going Jasmine." I mumble to myself as I slowly slouch in my chair.

It's finally lunch time and once the bell rang, I raced out of school. I arrive home and my mom says "Jasmine, do you have any homework?" "Yes mom, I do." I replied. She then tells me to get it done so I don't have to worry about it after school. I know my mom is just looking out for me and all but seriously? I have to do my homework instead of spending time with my friends? Totally not cool.

I sit at the kitchen table and recite my answers to my mom so she can write it down. I've been strictly homeschooled by my mom all my life up until high school. She never lets me touch pen and paper, or paper in general, or any writing tools. We always do homework verbally, although I'm not sure why, and I won't dare to ask. I am sitting at the kitchen table and my mom took my homework out of my bookbag and is reciting the questions to me so I can answer them aloud and she'll write it. As I'm answering the questions my mom tells me that she has to jump on a business call. I notice that there is a pencil and piece of paper near me. I examine the room to make sure nobody is watching and start doodling. My art is a little rusty considering the fact that I haven't picked up a pencil in a long time. So, I started to scribble dark clouds at the top of the page. I scribbled dark clouds because it represented how angry I was at my mom for not letting me hang out with my friends.

No more than minutes later, my mom stampedes down the stairs and once she saw me doodling, she looked completely astounded.

CHAPTER 4

"No, no, no no!" Mom panics. "MOM, what's wrong?" I say, flabbergasted. "P-put the pencil down, sweetie." Mom stutters as her voice softens. I drop the pencil and put my hands up as if the cops are about to arrest me, but the cop in this scenario is my mom and the jail is being stuck in the house for another 15 years, or however many years I've been trapped here.

Mom rushes to the window and watches the clouds shift from white to black. Then, she slowly turns around and says, "Jazzy, there's something you need to know." I don't say anything after that, but I am slightly confused. "So, you have…well, a gift." Mom says. "What do you mean by a gift?" I say, now wondering if my mom is keeping a secret from me. "Jazzy, you have powers. Whatever you draw comes to life. This is why I haven't let you touch pencil and paper since you were 7." Mom says. I am so shocked; I've had a power that I never even knew

10

about all this time? This is so cool! "Really?!" I say, trying not to smile, knowing that I'd want to try out a ton of things. Mom nods her head, then says "I know this sounds very cool and amazing, but now that you know you have to make excuses not to write on paper while in school. Bad things can happen. And don't go telling one of your little friends too." "Okay mom, I won't tell anyone." I say as I check my phone; the time is 1:50 PM, and lunch ends at 1:00. "Mom, can I go back to school, or do you want me to stay here?" I ask. "Of course, you can go back." Mom says, smiling.

CHAPTER 5

Back in School

So, I head back to school and Mia and Charlotte approach me. "Hey girl! Where have you been? Free period is almost over!" Charlotte says. "Oh um... about that." I start. "Wait, wait, wait please don't pull a "Jazzy" on us again. Don't tell me you're backing out?" Mia sighs. "Well, I can't paint with you guys today" I say looking down at the floor. "Come on, Jazzy! You're always dropping out on us! For my 12th birthday it was a spa day and you get to draw your nail style look you said you couldn't come because your mom said you were busy. And every single other time!" Charlotte says as she crosses her arms. "Exactly! You're never there for us Jazzy! What's going on with you." Mia says, trying to make eye contact with me. "I can't tell you guys." I say as my voice softens. "Of course. You can't tell the two people who've been with you your whole life!" Mia says, disappointed. I wanted to tell them

12

the truth but my mom said I couldn't. I feel like my conscience is telling me to not say anything but a part of me is saying to tell them. I just stay quiet hoping that they'd forget about all of this. "You know what, fine. Don't tell us why you can't paint with us. But if you can't tell your best friends what's going on with you, then you have no business calling us your best friends." Charlotte says as she swings her silky blonde hair out of her way. Charlotte then says "Come on Mia, let's go." Mia and I exchange glances then she runs off with Charlotte. Honestly, they kind of made this so dramatic, what was the point of making such a big deal out of the fact that I can't paint with them. Whatever. I head to science class and notice that class is already over because students are walking the opposite direction as me. Just great. Now I'm walking down the halls to go out of school. While walking, I pass the library and I peek through the windows and see Mia and Charlotte painting their hydro-flasks and canvases. I just sigh and keep walking. When I finally reach the outside of school I watch as the bus drives away. For some reason I didn't comprehend that I missed the bus for a solid 3 minutes. But when I did it the words "oh" were the only ones that escaped my mouth. I start racing like sonic to the bus. When I got there all of the students from different grades were staring at me as if I was a psychopath that chases after moving things because they don't have the ability to make it places on time and is always losing their friends because of their extremely strict mother whose homeschooled you nearly all your life making you seem like a crazy maniac. Oh wait. Maybe I am. Honestly, I'm never doing this again, I'll just walk home from school.

CHAPTER 6

The truth

The next day I go to school I try to approach Mia and Charlotte but once they see me, they immediately walk somewhere else. I started to follow where they're going till the point where I felt like I was chasing them. We are in a little alley in the halls and because I was so exhausted, I say, "Okay, okay. I give up! I just wanted to tell you guys why I couldn't hang out with you but forget it!" I say, panting. Charlotte and Mia then step towards me and Charlotte says, "Fine, tell us everything."

After I finish telling them everything their faces are in total shock. Except Mia didn't seem convinced, so she dug into her bookbag, grabbed a piece of paper and a pencil, then said "If this really is real, then draw us both chicken wings, french fries and a soda pop. I'm starving because I didn't eat the school lunch today, it was nasty anyways." "Uhm, Okay then." I say, laughing. But Mia's face looks serious. So, I take the paper and pencil and sit on the floor and start to draw. Charlotte and Mia then sit on the floor, and stare at me as I start drawing the outline of the food.

As soon as I finished drawing, Mia said "Well, where's the food?" And before she could even finish, a boy with black hair, orange shoes, and a black shirt striped with blue came up to Mia and said, "Hi Mia! Mr. Beckette told me to give this to you as an early birthday present!" The boy then hands Charlotte and Mia chicken fingers, French fries, and a soda pop. Mia slowly turns around facing me in shock. Mia then says "I hope that boy knows that it's the middle of May and my birthday is in February." I start to laugh then say "Told you I wasn't kidding." "Yes! Good food at last!" Charlotte shrieks as she gets up from the floor and starts to go to the macarena. Mia starts to laugh, then tells me and Charlotte that we are all late for class and should hurry up. So, Mia and Charlotte stop fooling around and quickly eat her food.

CHAPTER 7

Mia

So, in case you didn't know my name is Mia and as you probably already know, I'm Jasmine's FIRST best friend. I never wanted Charlotte to tag along when we met in the 5th grade because I knew that she would eventually meet Jazzy. And Once when she did, I felt completely forgotten, but it's all cool now because Charlotte and I have become pretty close friends. I've also been best friends with Jazzy since daycare, and whenever it would be art time or crafts time Jazzy would always jump to be the first one to start. I never knew why. But one day, she just stopped and her mom literally banned her from talking to me for a while. I always thought that I did something wrong, or that everything was my fault. The only way we got in touch was seeing each other at the grocery store. Eventually, Jazzy got a phone and we texted again and here we are. I knew that Jazzy loved art but, I didn't know that she would make this huge stupid lie as an excuse. Honestly, since she started talking about her having powers, I immediately knew it was completely bogus.

Just think about it, after Charlotte tells Jazzy that we couldn't be friends anymore she suddenly has magical powers. Doesn't that seem a little odd? And that situation with the food must've been a coincidence... But then again, what if she actually does have powers? She did seem quite serious when she explained it to Charlotte and I, and Jazzy usually twitches when she lies and she wasn't twitching when she told us…

Okay fine, well even IF this is true then… that's totally unfair! Why couldn't I have powers? Jazzy is a clumsy little girl and I'm so much more mature and better than her! She is always acting dramatic as if she's the main character and her life story is being written in a book. Wait…

You know what, if I can't have powers then neither can Jazzy. Although she's been so nice to me our whole lives it would be wrong to ruin her life. Meh, who cares. I don't know what my plan is exactly, but I know that Jasmine will wish that she never told us anything. Hopefully after that happens her powers will disappear and transfer to me! Boom, problem solved. Your powers will be mine Jazzy, just you wait.

CHAPTER 8

Charlotte

So, Jazzy has powers, Mia is jealous, and I'm just stuck in the middle. To be honest, I'm not surprised; Mia is the worst liar in history and gets immediately jealous if someone has what she wants, then she gets crazy. When I first met Mia in the 5th grade (before I met Jazzy) a boy asked to borrow her pencil. Mia said no and then the boy dug into his bookbag and found a pencil of his own. The boy's pencil had a bunch of cool glittery stars on it and its eraser was a big heart eraser. Mia saw the pencil he had and asked if she could have it. And because Mia said no to when the boy asked, the boy said no. Mia became very upset and waited till lunch to express her anger. It was now recess and while the boy was running down the stairs to go outside, Mia tripped him and he fell on his face onto the concrete floor. Mia nearly got expelled and probably would've if she didn't run away pretending that she didn't do a thing. But anyways, that's all I have to say. I'm just going to play it cool and nice and sweet until Mia tells me her plan. I don't know what Mia's up to, but I know Jazzy is in for something huge. I don't know what, but it's gonna be something. And when she does, I'm just going to be that girl in the corner eating popcorn and watching the whole thing.

CHAPTER 9

Art class Aftermath

After classes, it was finally dismissal. Though, I made the absolute moronic decision of my life while in class. I decided to try out for the art club, forgetting about my so-called "gift." My teacher said that tryouts were right after dismissal was over. So, now I have to go to the art room for tryouts. Just great.

While walking to the art room I think I saw Mia and Charlotte watching me. I was going to approach them but I knew that by the time I finished talking to them It would be 9:00PM. Then I would've missed the tryouts, which would've made me feel really bad. Instead, I have my eyes glued to the door with big bold letters in a rainbow that says "THE ART ROOM." So that I don't get distracted. I've finally gotten there and it feels like everybody is watching me. That moment is a perfect moment for Rockwell's song "Somebody's watching me" to play.

"Congratulations Jasmine, you're not late, for once." Mr.Paradora says. I usually don't say anything whenever a teacher does that, but for some reason I blurted out, " Congratulations for being late for literally everything. Mr. Paradora. You're never early for anything, even your dates, this is why Mrs. Babbly (The science teacher) broke up with you. And for a teacher your vocabulary is very limited considering the fact that all you know how to say is " Why were you late" or "Want to explain why you were late?". Pretty much anything about being late, this is why you're a stressed out, single man with no life, no family, and not even a well paid job-" I stop and shut my mouth quickly, realizing what I just said. Mrs. Muna, the new art teacher then came into the room. Oh shoot. Two teachers who are extremely strict just heard me say that. Maybe I went a little over the top... I just can't stand when teachers call me out for everything. It just makes me feel like I can never be good enough for them. "Excuse me?? Did I just hear what I think I heard? You cannot talk to a teacher like that young lady. Go to the principal's office. You can try out for art there." Mrs. Muna says while shoving a painting canvas and paint brushes in my face. " Go, go, go! Get out!" Mrs. Muna says scolding me, angrily. I take the canvas and brushes and go on my way. I think I'm in enough trouble already.

CHAPTER 10

Principal's Office

I am now in the principal's office re-thinking my life. What in the world was I thinking? But then again, they kind of deserved it. Anyways, Madam Josephine, the principal, was staring at her computer the whole time, and she'd only look at me if I asked her something.

A few minutes later, Madam Josiphine left the room because she said she had to " take care of business." Though, I could hear her talking to the other teachers and sipping coffee. A few minutes after she left, Mia and Charlotte walked in the room. Mia then grabbed the chair that I was sitting on and spun it around. " Uhm, yes Mia? And hello to you too." I say, laughing. But once again, Mia looks so serious so my smile fades immediately. Mia then let's go of the chair and her evil-ish grin turns into an innocent smile. "Hi Jasmine! So, would you like to be the most bestest of friends in the world by doing me a favor?" Mia says as she twirls her hair on her finger. " Well, if someone else were asking me this I would say no. But since you're my absolute best friend.. of course!" I say, smiling. Mia is the type to not ask for too much, plus, I trust her! So whatever this favor is I bet it's nothing. Actually, after school, I might treat Mia and Charlotte to something. In honor of keeping my secret and being amazing, loyal, friends. "Well…. I've always wanted to go somewhere but my parents would never let me because they said it is " too expensive" Mia says, as she looks down at the floor. "Oooh! Where are you thinking we should go? The park? Ice cream shop? Or….The zoo!" I say, getting up from my chair, excitedly. " Yes! The zoo sounds fun!" Charlotte says contentedly as she high-fives me. " No!" Mia yells. "Girls think bigger! I'm talkin'… PARIS!" Mia says with Jazz hands. Mine and Charlotte's smiles fade away immediately. " That sounds really cool, but how would we get there?" I ask, suspiciously. "Well, I was wondering if you could draw us there?" Mia pleads, fidgeting with her fingers. "Pleaseeeee!" " I don't know, Mia, that's a big favor." I say, kind of shocked. " If you don't then.. then I'll tell the whole school your secret!" Mia says. " Are you trying to blackmail me?" I say, as I cross my arms. "Maybe I am! Now do it or else I'll not only tell the whole school but, I'll also tell everyone on social media." Mia laughs, holding up her phone. I can't believe this, I thought Mia was my

best friend and she betrayed me..That kinda hurts. "
O-Okay fine." I say, stuttering. I sit back in my chair,
and grab a pencil and piece of paper that I see lying
around. I then drew stick figures of Charlotte, Mia,
and I in Paris. I drew the eiffel tower in the
background as well.

Within the blink of an eye, the Eiffel tower is right in
front of my face; with Mia and Charlotte beside me.
I have a bad feeling about this.

CHAPTER 11

Problems in Paris

"OH MY GOSH! We're actually in…Paris, France?!" I shriek, slightly excited as I'd hop up and down. " No way, no way, now way!" Charlotte says, jumping up and down with delight. " Told y'all this would be a good idea!" Mia says, satisfied. I just sigh and cross my arms, again. Mia then says " Well, now that we're here.. let's go and have fun!" "But we have regular money, not Euros." Charlotte says. "What's Euro?" Mia asks. "It's what people in France call money. I did my research." Charlotte says, proudly. "You were the one who wanted to come here Mia, I thought you'd know." I say as I glance at Mia. I'd have to admit, I am being a little sassy, but Mia deserves it. Mia just ignores what I said then says, " Well, Jasmine Johnson you're the one with the powers, why don't you draw us some money?"

"You mean like… counterfeit?"

"No!-"

"Are you trying to get me arrested?"

"Well-"

"That's against the laws Mia. You're trying to set me up to become a prisoner!"

Mia goes silent. "Umm, anyway-" Charlotte starts. " Why don't we get a hotel to stay at, in the meantime! If we find money." "Well, Jasmine. If you want your "best friends" to survive in a place that YOU put us in, why don't you get us some money? Now drawing it IS a really good option, but im not forcing you to..." Mia says as she gives a slight smirk. "Ugh fine! But if I somehow get in court then I'm putting y'all to blame." I say, annoyed. " But where am I going to get a paper and pencil from?" " Why don't we go in there?" Charlotte says as she points to a restaurant with the words "Jules Verne" on it. " I guess we could go." I mumble. " Great! Let's go!" Mia says as she races to the restaurant.

When we get there, a tall man in a black and white suit stands behind a counter. " Bonjour les jolies dames!" The man says as he gives a big smile. Mia leans over to me then whispers in my ear " What did he say?" " I don't know" I whisper back, slightly giggling. "I have a translating app on my phone! It can detect voices. Someone ask him to repeat what he said!" Charlotte says as she digs in her purse and grabs her phone. " Uh- uh- Bonjour! Mister..mademoiselle?" I giggle, nervously. The man tilts his head in confusion. Mia shoves me out of the way then says "Bonjour Sir! Me llamo Mia! Eh- could you repeta your selfa?" I aggressively facepalm." That's spanish you dingbat!" I yell, angrily. "I'm not sure I comprendre..." The tall man says. " I've got it!" Charlotte declares, happily. "He just said that he doesn't understand what were saying, which means he only speaks french! So, this is what we have to say:

"Vous êtes une mauvaise personne et devriez quitter votre emploi."

"Okay, though I'm not sure I'll pronounce it right, but I'll give it a shot!" I say as I study the translation on Charlotte's phone. I walk back up to the tall man and give a big smile, then I say "Vous êtes une mauvaise personne et devriez quitter votre emploi." Once I say that the tall man's smile fades immediately. "How dare you! Sortez! Sortez! Sortez!" The tall man says as he shoves us out of the restaurant.

"Great. Just great." Mia says, as she kicks a piece of chalk lying on the ground. "Thanks to Jasmine and her bad ways of communication we can't get money." "You mean Euro." Charlotte says. "You know what I mean!" Mia yells. I look down on the floor and notice that Mia is kicking chalk. "Wait, Mia stop!" I kneel down and grab the chalk. "My powers allow me to draw things and they'll come to life. Does that mean I can use chalk to draw money and it'll come to life?" I ask. "I guess." Mia says in a whining tone, rolling her eyes wishing she thought of that first. I start to draw big rectangles and little sketches of people. I draw what I think that money in Paris will look like. I draw a lot of rectangles, knowing that we'll need a lot of money. When I finished drawing, I got up from the concrete floor and turned around. "Euros!" I exclaim as I kneel down and clutch the money. Mia then walks closer to me and snatches the Euro right out of my hands then says "Alright, now that I have the money, let's go and book a hotel to stay at." "Okay! Not a problem, I'll search up hotels that we can stay at." Charlotte says, as she turns her phone back on and starts rummaging through the internet. No more than 3 minutes later, Charlotte exclaims "I've got one! It's really pretty too." ""Okay, what is it called and where is it?" Mia asks. "It's called "Hotel Ritz Paris, just take a look at these pictures! They look fire!" Charlotte says as she stares at her phone with awe. Mia and I both take a step closer to the phone to take a look. "Holla!" I yell. The both girls stare at me with confusion. 'Uhm, anyways! That hotel looks beautiful! But how will we get there?" I ask, looking in the sky. The sun is in my eyes, and at this point I'm desperate for an air conditioner and some cold water. Charlotte interrupts my thoughts by saying, "So we don't have a car, but we do have money to get one! I have a navigation app on my phone, it says that it'll take us about 20 minutes to get to the nearest car shop." "But none of us have a license." I say. "Alright, then I guess we won't be going to the car shop, let's just walk to the hotel. On my phone it says that walking to the hotel will also take 20 minutes!" Charlotte replies. "Okay then we best be on our way!" I say. "Lead the way, mademoiselle." Mia says as she bows her head down, acting as if she is a prince. Charlotte laughs and gestures to us to follow her.

CHAPTER 12

Problems in Paris

(Part two)

After 20 long, sweaty minutes we've finally arrived at the "Hotel Ritz Paris" The place looks huge! Mia looks completely mesmerized, Charlotte is scrolling through some social media app on her phone, and I'm just...well I'm the only one being normal right now. I honestly don't know why Charlotte is so obsessed with her phone; I think she needs to learn how to live a little out of the social world. But I guess it's okay considering the fact that she's the only LOYAL one around here.

Mia, Charlotte and I are all just standing outside of the hotel as we watch people come in and out. "Uhm it's too hot outside to be watching people pass, I'm going inside and asking for a room. Are y'all coming?" Mia asks in an annoying tone.

Charlotte and I don't say anything, we just walk into the hotel.

Once we got in the hotel, I let out a sigh of relief, it's so much cooler in the hotel than it is outside. They also have a chandelier! This place is amazing. Charlotte walks up to the person behind the counter. This time it isn't a man behind a counter, but a woman with blonde hair that looks kind of like Charlotte's, blue eyes, and a pretty blue beret. "Bonjour! That's French for hello! How can I help you?" The woman says. "Wait, you speak English? For real?!" Charlotte asks, happily. "Little bit." The woman says as she gives a big smile. "Okay so, me and my friends need a room to stay at." Charlotte says desperately. "Of course! How long will you stay?" The lady asks. Before answering, Charlotte walks towards Mia and I and asks how long we are staying for. "I don't know! Maybe for two weeks?" Mia asks.

"I was thinking two days" I started.

"Well, I said two weeks and that's final-" Mia says as she gets cut off by Charlotte.

"Guys can we finish this when we get the room? Thanks." Charlotte says, as she rolls her eyes and twirls back to the woman. "We will be staying for deux semaines!" Charlotte says, proud that she can speak a little French. "No problem!" The woman says as she starts typing on her computer.

A few minutes later, the lady escorts us to the elevator and clicks floor 10. When we arrive, the room smells of fresh, clean laundry. I love the smell of laundry detergent or clean laundry, and the room looks pretty too! "Here you go! Your new hotel room! Enjoy!" The woman says as she leaves the room. "Wow!" Mia says as she inhales deeply. "This place is amazing!" "I'd have to admit, it is pretty cool" I say, smiling. When you walk in the room there is a walk-in closet, which sits beside the door. Then, there are three full sized beds with fairy lights dangling from each one of them. There are also a variety of huge windows across from the beds. The windows also have a door which leads to the balcony, which has a large two-tier water fountain in the middle of it. I can't believe we could afford all of this!

After admiring the hotel for 8 minutes straight, Mia takes a step towards the windows and looks down. "uh…uh" Mia says as she starts to panic. "W-we're too high up." "Come on Mia, stop being a baby. You're fine." Charlotte says as she throws herself onto a bed. Mia starts to step away from the windows, then turns facing me. She then points her index finger at me and yells "You…You knew that we would be on a high up floor and purposely didn't say anything because you knew that I would panic!" "W-what? That's not true!" I say as I cross my arms. "Yes, it is. You know that I have panic attacks when I see heights, you're the first person I told!" Mia says as her face turns bright red. "I said that isn't true." I say, aggressively. "That's it, you're both psychopaths', I'm calling hotel security." Mia calls as she cat walks past me, elbowing me in my stomach. I was so close to just snatching those fake extensions out of her hair. Before Mia could walk out the door, a man wearing janitor's clothing stops her and says "Bonjour! Are you enjoying your stay?" "No, I'm not. This girl is trying to get me killed! Like a damn psychopath!" Mia yells as she points to Charlotte and I. "I'm sorry Madam but this is very inappropriate behavior, and against Hotel Ritz Paris laws, so I have to ask you all to leave this Hotel at once. "B-but that's not fair! I didn't do anything!" I say as I step closer to the Janitor. "Me either!" Charlotte calls as she hops off the bed. But the Janitor doesn't listen, he just points to the elevator, signaling for us to leave. So, Charlotte and I walk out of the hotel rooms with our heads hanging low. When Charlotte and I got into the elevator, I can hear Mia saying "Sir, can they leave and I stay? Please!" "Well n-" The Janitor starts. "I really love your work and your service; you always make the hotels smell and look amazing." Mia says. "Oh, well in that case of course you can stay." The Janitor says, flattered. "Thank you so much sir!" Mia rejoices as she'd embrace him with a hug. "Of course." The Janitor says.

I know she did not! I'm the one who got us here in the first place and she just ditches us? The audacity. And on top of that, Charlotte and I have to suffer in the heat while Mia gets to be lounging around in a hotel. While in the elevator I can hear Charlotte huffing and puffing. Charlotte then says "I can't believe her. She isn't even afraid of heights! She made that whole thing up so she can live in a beautiful hotel all by herself." I would tell Charlotte that Mia actually is afraid of heights but she seems to be venting off to me so I'll let her be. "I know right!" I say, rolling my eyes. By the time Charlotte and my conversation is over, the elevator stopped. Charlotte and I walk out of the elevator and the same lady that booked us a room watches as we leave the hotel in confusion. And here we are, back in the burning hot sun. " Now what do we do?" I ask as I have my hands on my hips. "Honestly, I'm tired, thirsty, hot, and am giving up on enjoying paris." Charlotte says, as she bows her head down in exhaustment. I look at the sky and notice that it's slowly turning into evening. "Why don't we treat ourselves to dinner, then I'll draw us a tiny motel to stay in for the night. Then we'll work things out tomorrow" I say, having pity on Charlotte. Charlotte sighs in relief as we both walk down the streets of Paris.

CHAPTER 13

Nighttime

When Charlotte and I finally arrive at what we think is a restaurant, we can see baguettes and croissants through the glass. "Mmmmh, those look delicious." Charlotte says as she licks her lips. "Yeah, let's head inside." I say as we walk inside. Thankfully this restaurant didn't involve too much communication, all we had to do was point to what we wanted on the menu, pay, and the cashiers would give it to us. Charlotte ordered two mini baguettes, twelve macaroons, and one jumbo croissant. " You must be really hungry." I say giving the cashier the money while laughing. " Yeah, I haven't eaten since school; plus this is Paris! I can't pass down the opportunity to try everything!"Charlotte says as she stuffs a macaroon In her mouth. I ordered a small pack of five macaroons, a small serving of waffle fries, a strawberry-banana smoothie, and a croissant for later. When I finished paying, I used half of the money we have all together. Charlotte and I thank the cashiers and head out of the restaurant. " Let's find a big open land of grass so I can draw us a motel." I say, while eating a macaroon. " Good idea." Charlotte says.

After a long walk, we've finally found an empty land of grass. I sit on the grass and pull chalk out of my pocket. I start to draw the outside of what I think a motel would look like, and I sketch the inside as well. When I put the chalk back on the ground the motel appears. I signal Charlotte to come inside. We are finally both inside and the motel is not the best drawing I've ever done but it'll last us. The motel has two queen sized beds, and two bathrooms. In Front of the beds is a large screen tv. I throw myself on one of the beds and drift off to sleep. Charlotte sits on her bed, turns on the tv, and munches on the rest of her macaroons.

Minutes later, we hear two loud bangs on the door. I pull the thick blankets off of myself and hop out of my bed. I walk to the door and open it. Oh no.

CHAPTER 14

She's back.

"Are you kidding me?" I say as I cross my arms. "Mia what are you doing here?" " I..uh." Mia stutters. " I'm listening." I say. " I got kicked out of Hotel Ritz Paris and have nowhere to stay!" Mia whimpers as a tear rolls down her face. "I'm sorry Jazzy! Please forgive me for everything I've done." Mia says, desperately. Mia has been a brat towards me and Charlotte, and caused a lot of trouble in Paris.. but... everyone deserves a second chance. I hesitate, then say" Okay fine, I'll draw you a bed; C'mon in." "Thank you Jazzy! Thank you, thank you, thank you!" Mia says as she pushes me out of the way and runs inside. I sigh and go inside as well.

While inside, I take a pen that came with the " thank you for staying" card. and start to draw on the card.

I draw a bed and within the blink of an eye, it's there. Mia didn't seem fazed though. She threw herself on the white and pink bed and began to scroll on her phone. I began to fall asleep and within a matter of minutes, I heard snoring as well.

CHAPTER 15

Done for the day.

Don't overuse your power.
You musnt tell anyone.

You can't.

Don't.

This could lead to serious damage.

Stop...

Stop...

STOP.

I gasp for air and lift myself from my bed. I quickly turn to my right to see Mia and Charlotte fast asleep.

I feel so sick. I started to get up and once I did, I felt so nauseous. Next thing I know, I'm in the bathroom, holding my hair, ready to retch. Oh, how I hate this feeling.

After 15 minutes of non-stop vomiting, I felt strong enough to get up. Which is when I see Mia and Charlotte staring at me. "Sorry guys, I'm not feeling too good today, as a matter of fact I was thr-" "Do I look like I care? I don't give one macaroon, 2 macaroons, red macaroons, blue macaroons!" Mia clarified. " Well you don't have to be so presumptuous 'bout it." I argued. "Presumptuous? What's this? ELA class?"

" As a matter of fact it should be, you obviously need it." I replied.

"Please, I bet you don't even know how to spell presumptuous."

" P r e s u don't know how to spell, which is why you wanted me to spell it!

" This is why you're a disappointment to your mom."

The room grew silent, till Charlotte replied.

" You better not lecture about her mom, you never even had one."

"Say one more thing and I'm abandoning both of you."

" Pssh, you think I'm scared of you? You think you're better than both of us? Huh?"

"Yes. I do. Very much, which is why I left y'all in that cruddy hotel."

"Oh please you act like you've been through so much. Charlotte and I almost passed out from heat while you were off gettin' ya nails done with the french."

"Well you-"

"Stop it, stop it, stop it!" Charlotte finally interjected. " Why can't we just enjoy a good trip without you two bickering at each other!" "Shut up Charlotte, you're not the main character." I'd say, throwing a pillow at Charlotte. "Hey!" Charlotte replied, throwing a pillow back at me. "Alright, alright, ALRIGHT! This is too much stress, I'm not getting high blood pressure for you guys." I'd start.

"Let's just…go home!" Mia screams.

_____

_____

CHAPTER 16

Going home.

"Yeah" Mia chuckles, " Let's get the heck out. You brought us into this mess, get us out, why don't ya?". " I agree with Mia, sorry Jaz, I wanna go home." Charlotte admits, staring at the floor. " Alright, fine. This is obviously too stressful for all of us." I replied. My palm wraps around the "thank you for staying" card. I draw my school, cars and stick figures of kids.

And within the blink of an eye…

I'm not there?

I'm not home.

Where am I?

WHERE. AM. I.

CHAPTER 17

"Sad and stuck."

"Where are we?" Mia retorts, sliding a hand on her hip. I squint so I can see what the sign says. "Francois Dupont High School?" I question. Charlotte immediately goes on her phone. "Guys.." Charlotte begins. "Yeah?" Mia and I reply. " We're still in Paris." Charlotte chuckles, nervously.

The three froze.

"Haha, no big deal, it was just a glitch, I'll just re-draw it! Heh.." I giggle, looking at Mia nervously. I put my hands on my pockets, repeatedly tapping them, trying to find the chalk. "Found it!" I say as I redraw our school. Nothing happened.

Oh no.

"Guys.. heh… we're stuck." I shiver, staring into their eyes.

"Haha, funny joke Jaz, now let's actually go." Charlotte laughs with disbelief.

" No, I'm not kidding. We're stuck." I repeat.

Charlotte begins hyperventilating, while Mia begins to panic.

"What do we do?!" Mia screams.